Lost Love Found in Eagle Cove

a small town Oregon romance story

by

M. L. Buchman

Cover images:
Young Couple In Love With Flying A Kite At
Countryside © Beznika | Dreamstime.com

Buchman Bookworks

Other works by M.L. Buchman

<u>Angelo's Hearth</u>
Where Dreams are Born
Where Dreams Reside
Maria's Christmas Table
Where Dreams Unfold
Where Dreams Are Written

<u>Eagle Cove</u>
Return to Eagle Cove
Recipe for Eagle Cove
Longing for Eagle Cove

<u>The Night Stalkers</u>

MAIN FLIGHT
The Night Is Mine
I Own the Dawn
Wait Until Dark
Take Over at Midnight
Light Up the Night
Bring On the Dusk
By Break of Day

WHITE HOUSE HOLIDAY
Daniel's Christmas
Frank's Independence Day
Peter's Christmas
Zachary's Christmas
Roy's Independence Day

AND THE NAVY
Christmas at Steel Beach
Christmas at Peleliu Cove
5E
Target of the Heart
Target Lock on Love

Firehawks

MAIN FLIGHT
Pure Heat
Full Blaze
Hot Point
Flash of Fire

SMOKEJUMPERS
Wildfire at Dawn
Wildfire at Larch Creek
Wildfire on the Skagit

Delta Force
Target Engaged
Heart Strike

Deities Anonymous
Cookbook from Hell: Reheated
Saviors 101

Newsletter signup at:
www.mlbuchman.com

1

Cynthia didn't make it down to Eagle Cove's beach very often anymore. It might have even been years. But it spread out before her from her deck perched on the high bluff overlooking the Oregon Coast so she didn't miss much that happened below. She could watch the long waves of the Pacific roll in from far away, stutter on the offshore reef and then break relentlessly on the beach. The drumroll of the waves onto the sand was the backdrop to her life that she missed when traveling even a mile inshore.

The cliff face gave her a true, on-the-edge

vista, but behind her the house and the deck would outlast her. Unless of course the big Cascadia quake struck and the whole bluff fell into the ocean, in which case she and the old house would go together. At ninety-four, such possibilities didn't worry her. Though she hoped her granddaughter wouldn't be home if it did happen.

At the moment, Skylar was tucked away in her bedroom nose to the grindstone, or at least to her computer. She was either trying to get a jump on college with her summer courses, or doing that social media thing with all of the boys who were ever hopeful about pretty redheaded girls. Cynthia made use of the opportunity to take her cane instead of the walker that Skylar always insisted on. She hated that damn thing. No matter how her great-granddaughter saw her, she wasn't old… only her body was.

She even had the wherewithal to take the fleece blanket off the back of the couch on the way to the deck. She'd have preferred to take the cable-knit cream-colored afghan that she'd made years ago out of thick Scottish wool. But to move that she'd have needed both Skylar's and the walker's assistance. The light fleece was all she could manage herself anymore.

The house was a blur of memories, though few of their objects remained. Hugh was gone, and he had been most of the memories, as well as their daughter Teresa. Knowing her time was getting short, Cynthia had taken care to give away or sell the things her great-granddaughter wouldn't want. At first it had been hard to let go of each possession due to the memories wrapped around it.

The agate she and Teresa had found on their last walk together down the beach before her daughter, then just Skylar's age, had left for college. And the ever so similar one from the last walk her daughter had managed before the cancer took her.

The model ship that Hugh had spent an entire winter building, and had stood on the bookcase for decades—with broken masts after he'd accidentally dropped a book on it that next summer. Weren't humans curious things. He'd been gone over twenty years, and throwing out that sinking ship had been one of the hardest things Cynthia had done.

It had taken her months, going through

these mementos one by one. Each time, after Cynthia had a fresh area cleaned out, she would set a few select items on the well-used maple dining table for Skylar to decide what she wanted. The girl had the good common sense to dispose of most of those as well.

It didn't matter really. This house wasn't about what was inside of it.

It was about the wall of windows that faced the wild Pacific. From here she had watched the soaring seagulls and the mating flights of eagles and ospreys. Ducks often paddled about in the small pond that Hugh had installed off to one side for just that purpose. Bird feeders attracted all sorts. The upside-down nuthatches contended with the ever so suave goldfinches with their upright posture and gold-and-black jackets. Feisty Rufous hummingbirds faced off the Stellar jays. The flickers were large enough to ignore everyone else while they clung and pecked at the blocks of suet. It was a whole world.

Unlike her younger days, it often took her half an hour or more to tend all of the feeders. Whether it was familiarity or impatience, the birds often fed from one feeder while she tended the next. Though the chickadees, which had always been her favorites, were the only ones brave enough to regularly feed from her hand if she cupped some seed in her palm.

The weather was always fresh here. The air swept ashore as if it had been invented in the mid-Pacific rather than sweeping in from Japan or Hawaii. It arrived in gentle zephyrs like today, or great wintry blasts. During the 1962 Columbus Day Storm, she, Hugh, and dear teenaged Teresa had retreated to the bedroom, peeking out occasionally from the front windows as they bowed under the pressure of the hundred-and-fifty mile-an-hour blasts off the ocean. They had cooked on the woodstove and read by oil lamps for weeks afterward until the electricity was restored, but the house had stood strong atop the cliff.

Every day was different and she loved them all. She'd miss that even more than she missed Hugh when she was gone. Of course she'd had twenty years to grow accustomed to Hugh's loss.

Today she especially wanted to sit out on the deck to watch the beach. Eagle Cove had few events that had survived the decades along with her. The annual kite festival was one of them.

A small breeze almost took the fleece throw out of her hands as she was settling at the small table close against the railing. She would take that as a good sign. Some years the wind didn't come, though that was rare here on the coast. Other years the rain came, and those were hard and sad. Everyone would arrive, but no one could fly.

This year brought warm sun and a growing breeze. Already dozens of kites were in the air and she could see more on the sand, preparing to launch. The excited shouts of children drifted up the cliff. Simple moments of joy.

Cynthia had first fallen in love with the kites of Eagle Cove when she was eighteen and thoughtlessly, deliciously young. Skylar at ten had been more mature than she'd been after finishing high school. The world of today was so different from the world of 1939.

2

Cynthia had first visited Oregon on a dare from her best friend.

"We're eighteen," Bea had said pointing at the advertisement in the *San Francisco Chronicle.* "We're single and we may never see each other again."

"That's because you are going to Vassar College. Do you even understand how far away New York is from everything?"

"Farther than Oregon."

Cynthia looked at the advertisement again. It was a small inset on the second to last page of the Daily Statistics section.

Redhead Roundup
in Eagle Cove, Oregon
Aug. 5-6, 1939
Beauty Contest
Most Freckles Prizes
Cutest Baby and more!
Skate by the Sea
at Hummingbird Roller Rink

It featured a drawing of a woman with long hair and a tight bathing suit diving into the sea. The entire advertisement had been printed in red.

"They put it on the same page as the listings about dead people."

"And newborns," Bea had protested. Her best friend would be gone ten days later. She was bound to meet someone back East. New York City was just a short train ride away from Vassar and Bea made it sound so exciting. Who knew if she ever would return. Cynthia was staying in San Francisco for college. It might truly be their last chance to have an adventure together.

So, Cynthia had climbed aboard a Trailways bus.

"See, it's a sign!" Bea had crowed with delight as she pointed at the red-and-yellow paint design. "Redheads. Red bus. Perfect!" Bea's favorite adjective about everything.

At first Cynthia hadn't noticed. But the farther north they rode on the winding cliff-side Highway 101, the more and more of the passengers had red hair. They had started with a half dozen of them in San Francisco, but two more had boarded in Bodega Bay, another three in Fort Bragg, three in Leggett.

By the time they crossed out of California, the bus was crowded with men and women all traveling to the Oregon Coast. There were women with hair so dark that red was only a bare hint. Others were carrot-orange, so bright that "red" didn't really apply. There was one boy who was certain that he had the Most Freckles contest already won; Cynthia didn't doubt him for a moment, he was more freckle than boy.

She became more and more self-conscious as they went. Her long red hair and fair complexion had earned her attention at the school dances; her proverbial dance card was always full until she had to beg off to preserve her feet from being worn to tatters. But aboard this one bus there was every variety of redhead imaginable. Big men who were Swedish in build, slender women with green eyes and Irish accents, and Bea with her stylishly curly mop who was comfortable in the center of every group.

Dizzy and sore from so many hours on the hard seats of the noisy bus, for they had ridden straight through, she let Bea lead her to a tiny cottage where five of them shared two twin beds and a couch. The couch was too short, but she had it all to herself and that was a relief.

3

Over the years, Cynthia had loved watching the evolution of the kites that flew above Eagle Cove. What they could now make with nylon fabric and plastic parts was magical. For years she had needed binoculars to make out the hand-painted art on the child-tall paper-diamond kites.

Now, even with her failing eyesight, there was no need.

The small triangular wing kites were quick, darting splashes of color and little more. Their wings snapped like angry bees in the growing wind. But the new kites were so large and rather than paint, the fabric itself was the kite-builders' medium.

A brilliant orange octopus was the first big kite aloft. Two stories high with cartoon eyes and eight long legs, it soon flew up until it was staring almost directly at her. She waved at the kite and fancied that the sea creature now floating in the blue sky waved its legs back at her.

A great spinner flew aloft next. It looked like a child's pinwheel built ten feet across with a dozen pointed tips all whirling about.

She could see the next giant kites being rolled out on the beach, but she didn't lean out to peek. Cynthia wanted to be surprised by each one as it lifted.

"Gran! You should have called me!" Skylar hurried out onto the deck. She was a surprise every single time Cynthia saw her. It was like looking in the mirror and seeing her younger self, but dressed in shorts and a tight-fitting tank top with no bra underneath that she'd never have considered wearing herself. Her great-granddaughter was tall, slim, and her shock of red hair tumbled over her shoulders just as Cynthia's had at that age.

Skylar hustled back inside and in moments the cozy afghan was wrapped around her despite the warm day. Her walker now stood close to hand and a cup of herbal tea rested on the table.

"Oh wow!" Skylar's attention finally swung out over the rail.

"Oh my," Cynthia couldn't help but agreeing. "I've always loved the whales."

A gray whale family of two adults and one youngster rose up from the sand. The kites were life-sized and while they'd been coming to Eagle Cove for a decade, they didn't often fly. The wind had to be strong enough to lift them, but not so powerful that they might damage the fifty-foot long works of art. And they were never brought out in the rain, of course. They slowly swam their way into the sky with long ripples down their flanks and lazy flapping of their big tails. The more adventurous half-sized youngster flew almost as high as the octopus that kept a cautious eye on the trio.

Soon there were frogs bigger than the ridiculous Lincoln Continental that Hugh had purchased in 1958. After all, how much car did a family of three need. "But it's beautiful!"

Hugh had been enamored. Giant squids rose into the air and creepy spiders with legs a story tall were offset by a car-sized puppy dog and a slender dragon as long as the biggest whale but instead ducked and weaved sinuously about the sky.

"It's magnificent," Skylar whispered out on a soft breath as she sat to enjoy the view. She dropped the fleece throw over her own legs and settled in to watch the show.

4

Cynthia remembered the Redhead Roundup more like photographic flashes than a continuous memory. It wasn't that her mind was going or the seventy-six years that had intervened; it was the nature of the weekend itself.

The big Saturday-morning, twenty-five cent pancake breakfast in the sparkling new Puffin Diner had to be eaten so quickly because the redheaded line at the tiny seaside café was out the door.

Splashing about in the cold water where the high tide had overridden the mud flats for the "clam-digging" contest. Prizes had been hidden beneath the sand in clam shells, but by the time the tide was down low enough on Sunday, no one could quite remember where the prizes had been buried. Most of the clams that were dug had been real ones which were cooked on the beach that night.

She'd been swept up by "Erik the Red" and the Coos Bay Pirates, much to Bea's frustration as she was left standing on the sand. The pirates' jokes at first seemed quite rude until she found the rhythm of their humor and decided that they were just being campy. They were pirates amidst a field of redheads after all; though she did wish that they pinched her behind a little less often. When she declined to kiss any of the "surly louts," they laughed but finally "set her free to wander the world in lonely solitude to pine after her time on the high seas." Cynthia noted that the next redheads they scooped into their celebrations were not so disinclined to accept the pirates' attentions.

She'd completely lost track of Bea, but did watch the boy from their bus indeed claim honors among the most freckled.

Bea found her again at the crowning

festivities for the Queen of the Redhead Roundup. Queen Norlene Haworth's smile was amazing as the dainty sixteen-year-old knelt in her white-satin gown clutching red roses while being crowned by the Secretary to the Governor himself.

"I want to be her," Bea whispered in her ear with a sad sigh.

"There's still the beauty contest tomorrow," Cynthia reminded her.

"You *have* to enter, Cyn. You're sure to win."

After her adventures with the pirates, Cynthia would enjoy less attention rather than more. At the night's big bonfire on the beach that was a problem as well. Ultimately she was the first to retreat back to their room. It was some hours later before the rest of her roommates returned. One of them, a girl named Julie Ann from some place called Wenatchee and who had very willingly joined the pirates' celebrations, never came back at all.

Cynthia was the first out of the room and on the beach the next morning.

5

*"**Look at that one,** Gran!"*

A scantily-clad mermaid fluttered into shape below. Her generous figure dressed in under-sized seashells and the green scales that sheathed her from the hips down left little to the imagination. But her hair was long and flowed as red as Sklyar's did and her own had so long ago.

That was what had captured Jerome's attention.

6

The sun had only just climbed above the bluff to strike the beach when Cynthia had ventured out into Day Two of the Redhead Roundup. It was still cool, so she'd worn a light shirt and slacks over her two-piece bathing suit for her walk. She hadn't particularly noticed the boy and his kite until she'd heard a soft, "Wow!" after she passed him by.

A glance back revealed that his attention was riveted upon her.

She arched her eyebrows at him, but instead of being cowed, he had smiled.

"Sorry, but your hair is gorgeous."

Cynthia had always tried not to be vain about her hair though she was rather proud of it. The boy's exclamation made her feel better than all of the pirates' gropings.

"And now," she asked, "that you see the face that goes with it?" She didn't know what prompted her to speak so.

"Even better," and again that wonderful smile. He was her age or near enough. He wasn't a big, strapping redhead like Erik the Pirate King. Nor was he some hollow-chested teen. He looked, she decided, nice. His mop of hair was a dark red and a touch unruly. Like it wanted a girl's fingers to comb through it.

And then she noticed his kite.

Dozens of kites had been flying over the Roundup yesterday. Simple box kites and diamonds had dominated. There had been a few more elaborate multi-level kites, including a terribly intricate one that looked like the original Wright Brothers craft.

But this one was an unusual design she hadn't seen yesterday. It was as if the box kite and the multi-tiered one had been blended together.

"That's a pretty kite." He'd chosen green paper and painted the balsawood supports brown so that it would look a little like a flying forest. "Does it fly well?"

"We'll find out if you help me launch it." He showed her how to hold it for launching. It felt both strong and fragile. The wind tugged, as if the kite was eager to fly.

Jerome walked hurriedly backwards, spooling out line as he went. He was so intent that when he caught a heel and fell to the sand, he scrambled back up showing no sign of injured dignity.

"Okay!" He shouted and pulled lightly at the now taut line. With barely a rustle it soared aloft.

It was hard to see it straight over her head, so she walked toward Jerome and she wasn't thinking about the kite. He was watching his kite avidly and he didn't look like a dip or a jerk. He simply looked very intent.

"Are you in college?"

"Uh-huh," he kept his eyes upward, so focused that he wasn't looking at her at all and now it was her dignity that felt a little offended. "Just finished my second year at University of Washington. I'm in the brand new aeronautical engineering department."

"That's like designing airplanes?"

He looked down at her in some surprise, "You know what that is?"

"Red hair means smart, not stupid." Cynthia replied, and almost walked away.

"Actually, red hair only means your parents or grandparents had red hair." Then he grimaced, "Sorry. I'm told that I'm a bit of a square about science."

Cynthia wasn't sure about the slang, but maybe she was a bit of a square too. Or else she'd still be in the pirates' clutches. She'd seen them romping up and down the beach followed by clouds of redheads. She would much rather be where she was.

"Smart is certainly nice though. Want to fly her?" He nodded toward the sky.

Before she could protest, he placed the ball of string in her hand. His hand overlapped hers until he was sure of her grip on it. A warm, strong hand that she missed as soon as it was gone.

The kite tugged strongly so she used both hands. It seemed that it was pulling at more than her hands, as if it was tugging at something in her heart.

"I never held something that wanted to fly so badly."

He reached out and she was afraid that he was going to take it back. Instead, he rested his hand over hers again, then pulled it in until he was almost touching her hip. The kite soared higher overhead, pulling harder as it climbed. Then he eased off abruptly and the kite fell and dipped. She almost cried out, before it resettled at the lower altitude and stabilized once more.

"Did you design it?"

"Sure did. I'm going to work for Mr. Boeing's when I graduate; that's what us locals call Boeing Aircraft," he clearly liked that inside bit of belonging. "They took me on as a summer intern this year. He is building the most amazing aircraft of anybody in the world. Why, someday nobody will take a train or a bus anywhere—you'll step on an aircraft and *whoosh!* You'll be there before you can say 'Jack Sprat.'"

She and Jerome spent much of the day down on the beach flying his kite. He talked about college. She felt a little ashamed about going to the new City College of San Francisco.

A two-year program to become a teacher didn't sound very important compared with designing airplanes. But he praised her saying that most girls he knew went to college only trying to find a husband.

When he went and bought them burgers and a Coca-Cola at the diner, he came back with a floppy hat almost the size of a Mexican sombrero.

"You're burning in this sun."

She'd noticed, but hadn't wanted to leave. It was nice that he'd noticed. Though she wasn't sure about wearing the hat. "You are burning as well, Jerome."

He pulled at the hat and she saw that there were two of them nested together. They looked ridiculous, but as they were both wearing them she didn't care much.

Jerome landed the kite while they ate. Afterward he fetched a paint set from a small bag he'd brought with him. He started painting on the kite's upper wing.

When she started to rise to see what he was doing, he shook his head.

"No. Stay right there."

That's when she realized that he was

painting her portrait on the wing. Cynthia was dazzled by more than the sun.

She barely heard the call for the bathing beauty contest farther up the beach.

"Hey! You should go. You're a contender, Cyn." She liked his nickname for her, though she'd never liked it before.

"Do you know what the grand prize is?"

He shook his head.

"A trip to the Golden Gate International Exposition. My friends and I are going to it next week anyway. I'm fine staying right here." And she was. Even more as Jerome inspected her over the wing of his kite again and again while he worked.

"Well, maybe this will change your mind." He lifted the kite and almost lost it to the wind sliding along the sand. She grabbed the ball of string to make sure it didn't get away from them.

He tried again more carefully. Then she could see what he'd painted. It was her, but not in floppy sunhat and a loose shirt over her bathing suit.

No, it was her as…

7

"Gran? Am I crazy or does that mermaid look like me?"

Cynthia shaded her eyes to look at the mermaid kite now climbing into the sky above Eagle Cove. It did look like Skylar. Actually it looked—

She had to hold a hand over her mouth to not scream, but some of it escaped anyway.

In a moment, Skylar was kneeling beside her chair. "Are you okay, Gran? Should I call the doctor? But how am I going to move you? Oh god, I should have gotten that wheelchair. I'm such an idiot—"

Cynthia moved her hand from covering her own mouth to covering her great-granddaughter's.

She managed only a hoarse whisper. "The kite doesn't look like you, sweetheart." She looked at it again in wonder, "It looks like me."

"But—" Skylar mumbled through Cynthia's hand.

"Trust me."

Skylar pulled her hand away, but held onto it tightly between her own.

"But how?"

Cynthia looked up at the mermaid now flying and dancing near the baby whale. She had no idea. But they were going to find out.

8

The trip down to the beach was an arduous one, but with Skylar's good care, Cynthia managed. There was no parking near the ramp to the beach, but Skylar got her seated out of the sun on the porch of The Puffin Diner then went to park the car.

She'd eaten a breakfast here seventy-six years ago. Now, Judge Slater, who ran the diner in his retirement, was kind enough to come out and offer her some ice tea while she waited. When he asked what had brought her to the beach, she didn't dare speak. There was such hope in the moment that she didn't trust herself. She could only pat his hand in thanks and watch the mermaid now flying high above The Flicker movie house.

Skylar returned with the walker.

In order to use it, she had to give Skylar the thin leather portfolio she'd kept in her bedside table all these years. It was one of the very last personal possessions she had.

"Don't open that, young lady."

"Whatever you say, Gran. Are you sure you're up to this?"

Cynthia looked at the ramp down onto the beach that ran alongside Grouse Hardware and didn't know, but she had to be.

Skylar was patience itself, cheering her along, and helping to move the walker forward through the softer sand. Every time Skylar asked if this was really necessary, Cynthia could only nod, conserving her breath for more effort than she'd expended in five years.

It took a long time and several rest breaks to reach where the kite lines from the mermaid descended into the crowd, but they made it.

The moment the crowd opened so that she could see who was flying the mermaid kite, she knew she'd been right.

A man in his forties and his son were tending the lines together. In the man's face, she could see hints of his grandfather. But in the boy's she could see Jerome reborn. Just like his long ago relative, he had little attention for them—all he cared about was the kite.

The man looked at Skylar for a long moment, the shock of recognition was as clear on his face as the confusion.

Unable to speak, Cynthia reached out a hand and tapped the portfolio that Skylar had carried. When Skylar inspected her cautiously, she tapped it again.

With a shrug, Skylar untied the string.

9

Jerome held the kite up for her to see.

Cynthia's face and torso had been painted across the wing. Instead of a bathing suit top, her image wore the scantiest of clam shells. Instead of the bottoms, she wore a long sinuous tail of shining green scales. But most off all, her long red hair billowed across the kite's wing.

Looking up from the beautiful image, made with an engineer's eye, she stepped up to him until they were separated by only the thin paper and balsa of the wing. She pulled his face down to hers and kissed him.

10

"It was a kiss that I'll never forget. A girl never forgets her first *real* kiss, no matter how old she is," Cynthia said the last to Skylar who only blushed in return. Young girls were kissed and plenty more these days, but by that blush she'd guess that Skylar still hadn't found the right man to make a memory which lasts a lifetime.

Thomas had settled her into a folding lawn chair and sat in another. He held the portfolio as he and his son Simon looked down at the painting within.

"Jerome finished the kite on the beach knowing he had no way to take it home once he had glued it together. It only flew that one day. As the sun set in the waves, right there," Cynthia pointed out to sea, "he cut out the painting and gave it to me."

Simon glanced up at the sky where the mermaid—where *she* still flew. "Dad kept a few things for me when Great-Grandpop died. The design for that kite was one of them. It was dated August 6th, 1939. It also had your first name on it and 'Eagle Cove.' Dad and I decided to try to build it and fly it in his honor. I was kinda named for the kite. Cynthia—Simon," even his shrug was so much like Jerome's that it hurt to watch. "Funny. Guess I was sorta named for you, lady. Now that's kinda cool. Named for Great-Grandpop's old girlfriend. I'm good with that."

And they all shared a laugh, though it took almost all Cynthia had left to join in.

She didn't know how to ask, but being an old lady, she knew she didn't have time to avoid the question either.

"He never came back," she told Thomas after his son had returned his attention to the kite. He was showing Skylar tips on how to manage the big kite and how they'd built it.

Cynthia had come back to the Redhead Roundup from San Francisco in 1940 and 1941, then they had ended with the war. After the war was won she moved to Eagle Cove and taught children for forty years. And every year she had watched the sky during the kite festival hoping to see that unique box kite. Her letters came back marked "Addressee unknown." If he ever wrote, the letters never reached her. Her parents had moved mere weeks after her return from the Redhead Roundup when she moved into the city for college. So many things had been lost.

"He was co-opted into the war effort right out of college," Thomas said softly. "Long before the war. He would have been in England then, helping with their plane designs. Very secret work. I'm so sorry."

"No. No. It's okay. I had a husband and a child. It was a good life. Apparently he did as well." She patted Thomas' hand and wondered which of them she was reassuring. Her life had come full circle. For she had come alive in a man's arms, right here on this same stretch of beach, ever so long ago.

Cynthia sat in the chair and watched Simon

and Skylar flying the mermaid that looked like her and her great-granddaughter.

They stood so close in the afternoon sun that the light didn't pass between them.

As close together as she and Jerome had once stood, flying a kite in the sky.

My apologies

My small town of Eagle Cove has stolen the twice-yearly Kite Festival from Lincoln City, Oregon, which indeed has a family of life-sized great whales. Eagle Cove has also laid claim to the "Redhead Roundup" from Taft, Oregon which was held as an annual fundraiser for the town on the first weekend of August throughout most of the Great Depression.

About the Author

M. L. Buchman has over 40 novels in print. His military romantic suspense books have been named Barnes & Noble and NPR "Top 5 of the year" and *Booklist* "Top 10 of the Year." He has been nominated for the Reviewer's Choice Award for "Top 10 Romantic Suspense of 2014" by *RT Book Reviews* and is a 2016 RWA RITA finalist. In addition to romance, he also writes thrillers, fantasy, and science fiction.

In among his career as a corporate project manager he has: rebuilt and single-handed a fifty-foot sailboat, both flown and jumped out of airplanes, designed and built two houses, and bicycled solo around the world.

He is now making his living as a full-time writer on the Oregon Coast with his beloved wife. He is constantly amazed at what you can do with a degree in Geophysics. You may keep up with his writing and receive exclusive content by subscribing to his newsletter at www.mlbuchman.com.

If you enjoyed this story, you might also enjoy:

Return to Eagle Cove (excerpt) -a small town Oregon novel-

"Almost home, sweetie."

"Oh joy," Jessica Baxter tried to clamp down on her sarcasm. It was a bad habit that worked fine in her social set back in Chicago, but sounded more petty with each mile they drove toward the Oregon Coast. She slumped down in the passenger seat of her mom's baby-blue Toyota hybrid. It still had that new car smell. As much as she'd dreamed of owning a hot sports car some day, she knew that she was enough her mother's daughter that this was probably the exact sort of eminently sensible car she would buy when her VW Beetle finally gave up the ghost.

Just like her mom.

Maybe she'd get it in red to be at least a *little* different.

Jessica sighed again, keeping it to herself so that she wasn't being overly offensive. Her mother was one of the many reasons that she'd gone as far away as possible for college and did her best to rarely return—she didn't want to turn into her mother and it was too easy to imagine doing so if she'd stayed in the small town of Eagle Cove, Oregon.

They were like twins separated by twenty-two years. The two of them had been able to trade clothes since Jessica hit puberty and had shot up to match her mother's slender five-foot-ten. Other than a very brief mistake of dying her hair black as part of a tenth-grade dare, which had turned her fair complexion past goth and into bloodless vampire, they were both light blond.

The one part of twin-dom that she couldn't seem to pull off even though she wanted to was Mom's casual-chic. Monica Baxter was always dressed one step above the world around her; not fancy, just really well put together. The closest Jessica ever managed was Bohemian-chic which wasn't really the same thing, but she'd learned to make it her own. Of course, Bohemian was easier on the budget and often available in consignment stores which had only reinforced her chosen style.

Jessica did her best to not regress as they drove up into the Coast Range that separated the beach towns from the rest of Oregon…and failed miserably at that as well. She felt as if she was rapidly descending back toward being a pouty, pre-pubescent twelve from her present urban and worldly thirty-two.

Why did crossing the Oregon state line always take twenty years off her intelligence?

Maybe it was only Coast County. Because of the landscape the Oregon Coast felt incredibly far from anywhere. The Coast Range topped out at a mere four thousand feet high, but only a half dozen passes made it through the three hundred mile range of rugged hills that separated the beaches from the broad farming and industrial realm of the Willamette Valley. The interior of the state might as well be in a whole other country for how little it had in common with where she'd grown up.

"It's so strange being back here," Jessica rolled down the window and sniffed at the air. The scents were so rich and varied that they tickled. Bright with pine. Musty with undergrowth. Damp. A first hint of the sea.

"Well, it has been four years, honey. That's bound to make it seem a bit odd. But I'm so glad that you came."

"Me too, Mom." Better. She managed to say it as if she meant it, however unlikely that might be. Chicago fit her like a…but it didn't. The city was…something she was not going to give a single thought to for the next eight days. If she didn't fit there and she didn't want to fit in Eagle Cove, Oregon, then where did she belong?

Jessica breathed in deeply this time, trying to clear her thoughts with the fresh air of the Coast Range and nearly choked herself on how green everything smelled. The harsh slap of the mountains was almost an affront. The two-lane road dove and twisted along narrow corridors sliced through towering spruce and Douglas fir trees. The babies were sixty feet high along the shoulder as the car twisted up toward the pass; the mother trees behind them were much, much bigger.

And it wasn't just the trees that were lush. As they wound deeper into the Coast Range, each branch became covered with mosses and lichens. It soothed her eyes, so used to towering concrete and glass, with a living tapestry of greens, golds, and silvers. Beneath the trees grew an impenetrable tangle of salal and scrub alder. Old barns on the roadside didn't have shingle roofs, they had moss ones; some of them were covered inches thick. Many RVs, left unattended in front yards for too long, had a sheen of green growth on their north side.

"I really want to hate this," the Coast Range had three times the rainfall of Chicago, often surpassing a hundred inches a year. She expected to feel the weight of all that biomass crashing down on her shoulders, but instead she noticed the start of a disconcerting lightness as if coming home was a good thing. Jessica did *not* like that encroachment of pending appreciation, perhaps even enjoyment, upon her *true* feelings. "But it smells so good. Like sunshine and new growth."

Her mother's laugh was amused as they twisted along the two-lane road slowly climbing up a narrow valley.

"I didn't mean to say that out loud."

"But you said it anyway."

"Not helping, Mom."

Thankfully her mother's laugh said that she had understood Jessica's response as a tease. Which it mostly was, partly.

Jessica didn't *want* to like coming back to the coast. She didn't have small-town dreams. That was the main reason she'd left Eagle Cove. She had big city dreams…which weren't exactly coming together for her despite her efforts over the last fourteen years. But scurrying home wasn't going to fix those. And the selection of men in such a tiny town was, to put it kindly, pitiful. Puffin High—

Why they hadn't called it Eagle High in Eagle Cove was a subject of heated debate by every single class.

Puffin High's problem was that she knew every male her age all too well. The only reason the town had its own high school was that it was too far away from everywhere else for busing to make sense. Her senior class had just thirty-four students. Grades seven through twelve numbered under two hundred. And she knew far too much about every single one of them.

Even more obnoxiously invasive on her sense of right and wrong, instead of dumping rain, it was a perfect day. The sun sparkled down revealing a thousand shades of green in the living walls that lined the road. The air coming through the open window was thick with pine sap and the gentle tang of rotting undergrowth. There was so much oxygen in the air that it made her feel a little giddy.

Yes, a perfect day, if she'd been alone…and still in Chicago.

"I could have rented a car and saved you the drive, Mom." Actually, her budget had been thrilled when her mother had offered to come and fetch her. Also, once in Eagle Cove there wasn't a lot of use for a car, except when the rain poured down. The whole town was only a few miles long and she could walk most places she'd want to go. As if there were any old haunts that she'd care to revisit. She'd made good her escape to Northwestern University's School of Journalism at eighteen but every now and then the town still sucked her back.

"Nonsense, honey. I'm always glad to drive up and get you. Besides, I needed a few things for the wedding."

"How many is this?" As if she didn't know. It took much of her journalistic skill to keep "that judgmental tone" out of her voice. Something her early teachers had dinged her on until she'd learned to eradicate it. But since she was regressing as they neared the coast, it was trying to make a comeback.

"Number four."

"Why, Mom?"

"Because I love the man." Her mother actually glanced away from the road to offer her a scowl. "I'd have thought that was obvious."

"It is. But you've divorced him three times."

"Because *your* father can drive a woman bat-shit crazy without even trying." They giggled together because that was an absolute truth about Ralph Baxter.

"I meant, why marry him again? You're both legal age, your daughter lives in Chicago," and wouldn't complain if she lived on another planet entirely. "Just shack up together. Then you can lock the door whenever Daddy becomes too much like himself."

Ralph Baxter was always getting caught up in monster projects. Without a word of warning he would suddenly rip out the entire kitchen, once on the morning before a dinner party, because he'd thought of a better way to design it. Or he'd start building a new boat from scratch in the middle of the driveway, rather than in the generous side yard, which blocked parking near the house for months.

"Oh, honey. I'm too old fashioned a girl to 'just shack up.'"

Which was almost believable, even in the twenty-first century. To hear Aunt Gina—who despite her name was as not-Italian as a pastrami sandwich—tell it, Monica Lamont had chosen Ralph Baxter as her sweet sixteen love. She'd never even shopped around. How 1950s was that for a woman who hadn't even been born then?

Jessica had shopped plenty, or at least

window-shopped. She'd found only a few men worth the cost of trying on for size. Definitely not a one worth taking home to keep. She might look like her mom, all blond, tall, and waiflike—which she kind of hated though the men seemed to like it—but inside she wanted to be like Aunt Gina.

Luigina Lamont looked nothing like her twin sister…or Grandpop…or much like Grandma for that matter. She was a statuesque redhead, in every voluptuous sense of the word and completely lived up to her name: Luigina meant "Famous Warrior." Her merry laugh slapped up against you at the most unexpected moments and constantly poked at your ticklish spot until you were curled up on the couch begging her to stop. Unlike Mom and her serial marriages to the same man, Gina brought home plenty yet had only tried to keep one.

That "unholy disaster" (as the family tales described it) had produced Natalya Daphne Lamont—Jessica's three-hour-older (and Natalya never let her forget it) first cousin and best friend. Just like Gina, Natalya didn't look like either her mom or Gina's brief husband.

Maybe that was hereditary on that side of the family to balance out how much Jessica resembled her own mom and their shared grandma. Jessica had a sudden flash of her own future daughter looking just like her… and felt the world spin just a little at thinking about children at all.

"If I hadn't seen her come out between my legs myself," Aunt Gina would announce loudly, "I'd have thought I adopted the kid. Maybe I signed up to be a surrogate then forgot all about it."

Mom blushed every time Aunt Gina let that one loose in public, without understanding that if she didn't, Aunt Gina would have stopped long ago.

"Such an exotic offspring deserves an exotic name. Natalya for the Russian Bond girl in *GoldenEye* and Daphne for du Maurier the romance writer, *not* the nymph who had to turn into a tree to escape that lusty jerk Apollo." The fact that *GoldenEye* hadn't come out until Natalya had already been in grade school hadn't changed Aunt Gina's story one bit.

Maybe Jessica's own child would be lucky and take after Cousin Natalya who was slender like Jessica, but had all of the curves Jessica had prayed for throughout her teenage years but never been granted. Natya was also dusky skinned like a permanent tan and leggy like some French model. Jessica's and her mom's fairy light hair and Aunt Gina's mass of red curls had been transformed to a smooth cascade of dark chestnut on her cousin. Yet she and Jessica felt like twins from different mothers: one light, one dark, but much the same on the inside.

Jessica smiled at the sign as they cleared Maxine Pass: eight-hundred and three feet according to the sign. The "three" always made her laugh. It was like Becky, her other best friend from Eagle Cove, firmly insisting that she as five-four "and a quarter" as if it made a difference.

Maxine Pass was technically Maxwell Pass. Or it had been until the day that Aunt Gina had declared it just wasn't right for all of the passes to have male names merely because men were the ones who drew the maps back in the 1800s.

For her sixteenth birthday Jessica hadn't received her first kiss—already happened a year before—or gotten laid—two more years until that event. Instead, she'd been recruited for a "Mission!" At two in the morning on their shared birthday, Aunt Gina drove her and Natalya up to repaint the Maxwell Pass highway sign to Maxine. It had become a traditionthateverytimethehighwaydepartment changed it back to Maxwell, the three of them would have a two a.m. gals' outing and change the sign once again. The highway department had given up years ago. A few of the more recent road maps had even changed the name.

"Girl Power!" they'd shout after each time they finished repainting the sign, usually about three a.m. Then they'd break out the thermos of hot chocolate and drink it from a shared cup while they admired their handiwork by moonlight.

One time Martin, the town cop, had shown up while they were doing it. Jessica and Natalya had ducked, but Gina hadn't slowed down a single brush stroke.

"Thought it would be you," Martin had observedthroughhisopencarwindow,obviously talking to Gina.

"Out of your jurisdiction, Marty," had

been Aunt Gina's awesomely calm reply. She had always been Jessica's hero, but that totally clinched it. The town limits had been left far behind.

He'd joined them for the hot chocolate and had a good laugh at the "Girl Power!" chant.

Today Jessica just waved hello to the sign as they crested the pass and began their descent.

"Didn't you ever bust out, Mom?" Jessica tried to imagine her doing so, but couldn't quite conjure it up in her mind.

"Bust out? You mean cheat on your father? Never!"

"But what about between times, when you were divorced? That wouldn't be cheating."

Monica Lamont's lips thinned as she tightened her jaw and finally shook her head in a sharp little snap. "I was only living in the other end of the house."

"What about with Dad? You and Dad could just…you know?" The thought of her parents having sex was uncomfortable enough that she couldn't quite say it aloud.

"Ralph says that if I feel so strongly about things that I have to divorce him, then I shouldn't be expecting any special concessions while we are divorced."

Jessica felt she had to side with Dad on that one. He'd become used to his wife's antics, but that meant he didn't get any either in the interims. No wandering for him—it had always been clear that Ralph Baxter was absolutely crazy about Monica Lamont. Jessica felt kind of sorry for him.

"Wait. You mean you haven't had sex in two years?" This latest was their longest divorce yet.

Again that little snap that made Jessica's neck ache in sympathy. Mom moved to the right as the road added a climbing lane to reach the six-hundred and thirty-four foot (not quite so much bragging) Rogue Pass. That name at least made perfect sense by Oregon standards...because it wasn't anywhere near either of the two separate Rogue Rivers in Oregon. A half dozen cars roared past. Mom always drove exactly at the speed limit instead of the nearly mandatory ten over that prevailed throughout the state.

"So you're waiting for the wedding night?"

This time her mom's nod was a little sad.

"I'm sure tomorrow will be a great night, Mom."

At that she smiled brilliantly. "If the past three are anything to judge by, yes, it will be. It's just too bad we had to delay it."

"Delay it? Wait! What?" Jessica bolted upright in the car seat and almost throttled herself with her seatbelt. The wedding was supposed to be *tomorrow*. She'd secretly planned on staying just one day past the wedding, and then catching the Airporter Express that wandered through the small coastal towns once a day. She'd already warned Natalya to expect her in Portland for the rest of the week until her flight back to the Windy City.

"Well, we were meeting with Judge Slater about the ceremony. As he performed the first three weddings…"

Jessica resisted pointing out that he'd done all three divorces as well. Maybe her Oregon civility was coming back. Yeah, like a toothache.

"…and he had all of the old records in a file; even had the new marriage license pre-filled out, the dear man. However, it turns out that the first time we were married was on July fourteenth, not July seventh as I had always remembered. You know how your father loves the cycle of things. So we moved the wedding to next weekend to coincide properly with the original. I knew you already had your plane tickets, so I didn't see any point in telling you."

Didn't see any point? She'd have moved heaven and earth to— Actually, her mother was right because she'd purchased the cheapest non-refundable, non-changeable tickets she could find.

A week! She was going to be trapped in Eagle Cove from Friday morning until Sunday morning nine days later? Oh, that was so bad.

"I can't believe that we celebrated it wrong for all of those years," her mother continued, completely oblivious to the panic she'd just created. "The seventh was the date that had always stuck in my head for our anniversaries."

Mom's dropping voice spoke volumes. She'd always been terrible at keeping a secret.

"So why *did* the seventh stick in your head?" Jessica kept it as casual as she could, rather than rubbing it in that her mom always gave up whatever she was trying to hide. It must be the journalist in her coming out: ask the question and then wait patiently for a reply. Not pushing was another change between them. Jessica didn't feel as if she was mellowing with age, but perhaps she was. Being disillusioned at thirty-two was no more newsworthy than it had been at twelve or twenty-two; but a woman shouldn't mellow until…well, maybe a hundred-and-two.

On the back side of Rogue Pass, Mom concentrated on the winding descent. Jessica waved at a massive Roosevelt elk who grazed in a small clearing beside the road. Coming back to Eagle Cove might be only one step better than a nightmare, but it was a very scenic one. The road was soon joined by a stream rushing in a deep ravine on Jessica's side of the road; the problem was that they were both racing in the wrong direction—toward, not away from, her childhood home. The stream tumbled along almost as fast as they did down toward Eagle River which would eventually define the end of town where it opened into a broad bay before it reached the sea.

No one quite knew why the bay had been

named a cove, but it showed that way on even the oldest maps. It gave the town an off-kilter personality to Jessica's mind, as if it was always seeking to find its true identity. No bridge crossed the Eagle to the wilderness area on the other bank. To reach that required either a boat or an hour drive back up to Highway 101, across the river, and then a long crawl back to the Coast over marginal logging roads.

"C'mon, Mom, give." Since not pushing at her mother had failed, Jessica went with regressing and shifted to the wheedling tone she'd perfected as a child. She might hate herself in the morning for slipping back into it, but it always worked. Sure enough, her mom gave in right on cue.

"July seventh was the one time we cheated. We didn't actually wait for our first wedding night," the blush on her mother's fair skin was almost bright enough to lighten the dark corridor between the towering trees. "Your father made it amazing. But that's also the day I became pregnant, though I didn't know it until after the wedding. All those years I was celebrating the wrong date. That's why we never fool around unless we're married."

"Sounds like you were celebrating *exactly* the right date, Mom." She tried to pin down the exact date of her own first time, but it hadn't been all that memorable. Good, but "earth-shattering" was just another one of those 1950s' myths that didn't happen in the twenty-first century. Except, apparently, for her own mother. How unfair was that.

"Maybe," her mom admitted, "but we're going to get married on the fourteenth anyway."

"So, I'm a bastard?" Not that it bothered her, but she couldn't resist needling her mother about it. Maybe she hadn't matured all that much.

"Yes dear, but only by one week. I swear I didn't know." This time Jessica heard that her mom's confession was a sigh at Jessica's question rather than sounding contrite. Maybe it was time Jessica grew up a bit—even when in Eagle Cove.

"Does Aunt Gina know about all this?"

"No one does, except your father and now you. You only arrived three days early, which was actually four days late. No one gave it any thought."

Excellent!

To hell with being mature. Aunt Gina would love the extra dirt for teasing her sister and Jessica couldn't wait to be the one to tickle her aunt's funny bone.

# # #

It had been another long morning of assisting the Judge—always with a capital J. Monday through Friday, six a.m. to ten, Greg Slater helped his father. At first it had been something that Greg did to help out, but he'd come to like the simple routines and structure to his mornings.

"Ready?" he called back to the kitchen as he did every day. There was no real need to ask. The big old clock hung high on the wall said it was exactly six a.m. and the Judge was a very punctual man.

But Greg looked for the solemn nod before moving out into the diner and flicking on the fluorescents, "The Puffin Diner" sign, and the porch lights. There wasn't much need for the last, sunrise was twenty minutes ago, but the sun itself wouldn't clear the Coast Range ridge until at least six-thirty. For now, Beach Way, the town's main street, was mostly cool shadows and darkened buildings.

The bell mounted on the back of the door rang almost right away as Cal Mason Jr. came in. Greg had already set a mug of coffee on the counter for him. Cal ran the Blackbird Bakery and was hours into his day. Five days a week he was as punctual as the Judge. Cal Sr. wouldn't be in for a few hours yet.

"Your standard, Cal?"

"Double," though Greg knew that was a joke. Cal was one of the few men in town big enough that he could have eaten two of the Judge's generous portions. Six-two and as powerful as a bulldozer; his hands dwarfed the coffee mug.

Because Cal sat at the six-stool wooden counter, the Judge was less than five feet away through the broad service window that connected the dining room with the kitchen, but he waited for Greg to fill out the order slip and clip it to the spinner.

It was Greg's own damn fault. The diner's service had been a bone of contention, or rather "lengthy negotiation" just as most things were with the Judge.

"They can pick up their own damn plates at the window. Coffee pot is right there behind the counter where anyone who wants a refill can get their own."

Greg had won that round by subterfuge. He'd numbered the tables and then only put the numbers on the order slips, making it impossible for the Judge to boom out with "Veronica, your order is up." Customers had slowly adapted to not having to leave their tables for every little thing.

At least Greg thought he'd won, until a full three weeks later his father had winked at him while sliding across a short stack with bacon and hash browns for Karen Thompson, "Like I don't know who orders what on a Thursday."

Now the Judge wouldn't cook a thing without a proper ticket. Well, he'd cook it, but he wouldn't serve it no matter how busy or harried Greg was.

Cal's plate came up less than thirty seconds after Greg hung the ticket just as it did every morning: western omelet, hash browns, farm sausage, and English muffin. The last was about the only kind of bread that Cal didn't bake.

"Gotta have something that I can order out for and enjoy without baking it myself."

Greg moved the plate across to the counter and refilled Cal's half-drained mug of coffee.

There wasn't much call for a judge in a town the size of Eagle Cove. Semi-retired for the last five years, he no longer spent three days a week in Newport to sit on the bench as he had throughout Greg's childhood. Instead he'd set up a small courtroom in town. He mainly handled family matters like marriages and estates, and fines for drunk and disorderly tourists who soon learned that Judge Slater was a fierce protector of the town. There was only the occasional speeding ticket—no matter how hard Martin the cop tried to catch someone. The town was perched against the Pacific Ocean at the dead end of a winding two-lane that had left the coastal highway a dozen miles back; it had enough "Sharp Curves Ahead" signs to quell even the most lead-footed of souls.

So, "for something to keep me busy," the Judge held office hours only in the afternoons because his weekday mornings were all spent working as a short-order cook. And ever since

Greg's return to Eagle Cove three years ago, he'd been his father's front-of-house man: waiter, cashier, and busboy.

The Puffin Diner had been a near derelict before his dad had bought and reopened it. It was a classic small town place built to serve the early morning fishermen, especially those returning from a long night's work on the offshore shoals; it was little changed over the last ninety years.

The clapboard building stood high enough on a heavy stone foundation that even the Christmas storm flood of 1964 had crested two steps below the front entry. It was one of the only structures on the town's main street that didn't have a street-level entry. All of the other businesses that had existed then had high-water lines drawn halfway or more up their walls.

The Grouse Hardware store, the lowest spot in town close beside the docks, had a small wooden plaque of a fish screwed in just above the main door lintel. It was bright yellow with "Dec 22, 1964" painted on it in tropical blue—it was generally considered to be a little boastful, but old man Jaspar refused to tone down the color scheme that he'd painted on that fish in his youth.

The interior of the diner was so retro that it would have been ironic-modern if it wasn't quite so authentic. The steel-edged tables of blue Formica were scuffed nearly colorless by the thousands of plates and silverware settings that had been slid across their surfaces over the years. The chairs' red leather was sun-faded and the old chrome had pitted with rust from the salt air, making them uncomfortable to the touch without quite being painful. The linoleum floor had been replaced…back in the 1980s when mauve and hunter green had been trendy colors. The six round stools bolted to the floor at the counter squealed every time someone spun on or off them. The kitchen was authentic right down to the large service window, the steel spinner rack for order slips dangling in one corner, and the big grill and burners in the back. The scents of eggs, hash browns, and frying bacon filled the main street each morning enticing all passersby to come and find comfort food.

Ralph Baxter and Manny McCall came in and took their usual spot by the corner window.

They'd have tourists out fishing off their boats within the hour and were both after black coffee and tall stacks.

At first Greg had resented serving the Judge's fare—it was as invariable as his father. Scrambles, omelets, pancakes—no waffles because the iron had broken the same day Mom had died and he couldn't seem to fix it and wouldn't let Greg try. The pancakes were big and fluffy. The very crispy hash browns were not an option; they were on every single plate, even with the pancakes. Farm fresh sausage or bacon was the other staple on every plate—not that it was a choice. Everyone received whichever Carl Parker had delivered the day before along with the eggs.

All of Greg's efforts to vary the oatmeal recipe, served with bacon or sausage and hash browns of course, had been in vain. The Judge served only rolled oats—not steel cut—with sliced, not diced, dried apricots and diced, not sliced, fresh apple. Whether brown sugar or maple syrup was used to sweeten it was wholly up to the customer; local honey was also available.

Omelets were the Judge's real specialty and

by six-thirty there were already a dozen slips up for them. Omelets were the only dish where variations were allowed. He offered them with cheese, mushrooms, or smoked salmon fillings. Never all three of course, because there were limits to what was proper.

The Puffin Diner mostly served coffee. Greg's sole triumph at adjusting the menu had been when he managed to switch from Dad's "fresh ground" granules purchased in large plastic tubs to fresh-ground French roast. Tea or hot chocolate were the only other options, but asking for marshmallows with the latter was frowned upon unless you were a kid—the whipped cream came out of a spray can.

They'd fought royally over the Judge's in-flexibility, but of course fighting over things was a tradition in the Slater household. Not that voices were ever raised, because that would never do. The few times Greg had tried that tactic he'd been ruled "Out of Order" and banished from the dinner table: the sole forum for Slater "discussions." With Ma gone to cancer three years before—Greg's original reason for returning to Eagle Cove—he didn't have the heart to "force" the Judge into driving him from the table after that first time. When he'd been remanded to the kitchen two weeks after Mom's funeral, he'd made the mistake of glancing back as he'd moved off to finish his meal. His father had looked old, sad, and impossibly alone.

Greg hadn't been able to face living in the big old house out on the beach, so he'd moved into the guest house. Once he finally understood that no number of cogent debates were going to sway the Judge, Greg had let the menu go. It had been unchanged in either content or price in the last decade—other than the wavy black line of magic marker through the "Waffles (with blueberries when in season)."

Greg had been on the verge of leaving town when the Judge sat him down at the big house's dining room table. Ma Slater had been in the ground for a month. Greg knew he didn't really have anywhere to go, he'd learned all he was going to from the banquet chef at the Sorrento Hotel in Seattle and there weren't any top positions open for an untested executive chef wanting to make his mark. He didn't have the capital to make his own splash, not in the insanely competitive restaurant markets in the big cities. But he'd find something.

"Been watching you, son. Been tasting your food," the Judge had tapped a fork on his dinner plate. Greg had roasted a pair of fresh-caught trout in hazelnut butter with a dressing of spring greens and homemade basil vinegar. Though Greg had cooked half the meals since Ma's funeral—"fair is fair" the Judge had declared—it was the first time his father had spoken of it.

"Uh-huh," Greg had gone for a neutral acknowledgement. He knew the Judge hated such prevarications, but Greg didn't know where this was heading and went for caution.

"This is good. Damn good."

Greg hadn't been able to offer even a neutral grunt over his surprise at the Judge's remark.

"Still needs some work, though."

Before Greg could snap at him about what did a man who scrambled eggs and ruled on law know about fine cuisine, the Judge continued.

"You need more seasoning," and he aimed a fork at Greg's chest, "and I'm not talking about salt. Your technique is the best I've ever seen, but I don't taste anything special. There's nothing here that isn't in any other fine restaurant. You need time to find your own voice, not some other chef's."

"My own voice?" But he didn't need to ask, he'd heard it a thousand times growing up.

The Judge looked down at the trout, one of the only times he'd ever said anything without looking at whoever he was addressing straight in the eye, "Your mother taught me that."

Ma had been a painter, a good one. Her seascapes had sold in galleries up and down the coast. Tillamook, Newport, Gold Beach, they all snapped up as much as she could produce and was willing to let go of—Grosbeak Gallery in town had always gotten first pick though. She'd often talked about finding your voice in your art so that it didn't look like everyone else's.

"So, here is the deal I'm offering you."

Greg knew that it wouldn't be open to negotiation; no one negotiated one of Judge Slater's "deals."

"The diner is mine on weekdays from six to ten every morning. I'd like you to stay as my assistant because you're good at it. That pays rent here at the house, a small salary, and we split the tips. What you do with the diner for the rest of the time, that's up to you."

And for three years, Greg had stayed in Eagle Cove and searched for his own voice. In the first year, he'd never cooked for anyone but himself and his father—who never again spoke about the food itself. Then one night Greg had invited a couple of buddies from high school who were still in town to the diner, as a test audience. Word got out about how good it was and folks had started asking when he'd do it again.

He'd eventually started "Irregular Friday Dinners at The Puffin." He only opened when he had a new meal to test. It was all *prix fixe,* fixed price—a twenty in the jar—and a set menu. After two years of those he felt almost ready to take his cooking out into the world; maybe spend a while as a pop-up restaurant— there and gone—rather than a full launch. He'd been saving his half of every morning tip and every goddamned cent for when he went back to the cities. At first he'd simply been trying to be better by the time he left Eagle Cove, but he'd become obsessed with finding and perfecting his "chef's voice." He wanted it to be so clear that it was undeniable. When he went back to Seattle, no one would label him the protégé of Charlene at Maximilien's or Angelo at The Tuscan Hearth. He'd be his own—

The old brass bell screwed into the top of the diner's front door rang like a small ship was coming into port. Morning service peaked as usual around eight and had now tapered off to just a few lingering diners.

Greg glanced at the big-face clock above the cash register—9:57—and suppressed a groan. Judge's rule was that if you were in the door by ten, you could take as long as you wanted. If it was ten sharp plus a second, you were turned away—"Fair is fair." Maybe they'd be quick; he'd had an idea for a savory roulade that he wanted to try out.

Greg turned back and had to blink, then blink again. The morning sunlight shone through the front window and silhouetted two dazzling blondes, their hair practically set afire by the sunlight streaming in from behind them.

Then his eyes adapted as they moved farther into the room.

Mrs. Baxter who was soon to be Mrs. Baxter once again.

And a woman he hadn't seen since the day she'd left for college, but he'd know anywhere.

Jessica matched his own five-ten and her hair, instead of being the waist-long fall he'd remembered, now floated about her shoulders in choppy wisps that framed a face of high cheekbones, full lips, and eyes that sparkled with mischief.

Halfway across the old linoleum floor, she stopped and looked at him.

"Greggie's gaping, Mom."

And he couldn't do a thing about it.

# # #

"He is, dear," her mother replied cheerily.

"Does he do that to you a lot?" It was starting to get unnerving. In very short order, it would start pissing Jessica off. He'd been three years behind her in school. She'd dated his older brother for a while—he's the one who earned her first kiss at fifteen, but not all that much more. Her prior visits home hadn't overlapped with either brother being here, though she'd eaten the Judge's breakfasts before and had been looking forward to some comfort food since they'd turned west across the Willamette Valley. Her lemon-curd brownie from Loretta's in Chicago was many hours behind and much too far away.

"I don't think he's doing it to me, Jessica."

"Well, it had better be us and not just me. We are two fairly dazzling women after all. Besides, if he does it much longer, he's likely to get a dinner plate cracked over his skull."

Greg Slater shook himself like a wet dog and replaced his gape with a cautious smile. He'd done a lot of growing up since she'd last seen him. The gangly kid—who'd spent large portions of his freshman year in the principal's office—had turned into such a decent-looking guy that she might not have recognized him if they'd passed on the street.

"Hi, Jess."

"Jessica." Her high school nickname was one of the things she'd left behind along with Eagle Cove. She and Jessie Hamilton had been in a lot of classes together and everyone had called them both Jess despite their opposing genders. "I'm not a man, so don't expect me to answer to a male nickname."

"No you're definitely not—" she could see where his eyes were going, along with his smile. She gave him a second to recover, then two. She didn't give him three.

Jessica picked up a dirty plate from a freshly vacated table. It had a pool of syrup and a large splotch of leftover ketchup on some crispy hash browns. With a quick grab, she captured both the front of Greg's apron and his belt— maybe his underwear as well but she wasn't going to think about that. She tipped the plate into the space over his flat abs and managed to shove it half down his pants for good measure.

Jessica ignored his squawk of protest, letting go as he backpedaled away and almost landed on Cal Mason Sr.'s lap right in the middle of eating his tall stack.

"Let's sit over there, Mom," she waved hello at the Judge before they sat down. He flapped a spatula back in her direction.

The Judge never whispered, so she and the half dozen other late morning diners could hear him clearly when he told Greg, "Lady's got your number but good, son."

Did she ever.

Greg had been a real slouch, the classic

underachieving little brother. A decade and a half later and he was still in town working as a waiter for his dad. He'd grown up lean and dark. His neat black hair hung to his collar and the close-cropped beard accented a strong chin. He'd have looked Keanu Reeves' dangerous if it wasn't for the easy smile that still hadn't quite gone away. Greg Slater had come a long way from being fifteen…other than being another Eagle Cove failure-to-launch kid.

The last time she'd seen him, he'd been just starting his sophomore year in high school and panting after Dawn something—the hussy of the class. They probably had a trailer down at the end of Shearwater Lane that was slowly returning back into forest in a state of semi-decay, with a half dozen little Greggies bouncing about.

Maybe she should track down Greg's big brother Harry when she returned to the real world. Last she'd heard he was still single and practicing law in New Orleans…not that she was that interested in living in New Orleans, but it was a great place to visit. Maybe have some fun while she was there. She could even set up a few interviews in the jazz clubs and then write off the trip as well as selling a couple of articles to the trades. A couple of human interest stories, maybe find something unique enough to turn into a feature as well.

Though that was getting harder and harder. A few years ago she'd been able to get an article by the *Rolling Stone Magazine* editor way more than twice a year. And AAA used to give her bimonthly space in their magazines, but that had dried up as well. The collapse of print journalism was finally catching up with her.

Maybe if she'd been a straight newsie, she'd have stood a chance, but she wasn't. She'd always enjoyed the special interest story. Someone or some place that had found a way to be exceptional. A hot band, an innovative inventor, an amazing kid…those were the stories that had fascinated her. They'd shaped her career. And now they were "fringe" stories that didn't command much share in the shrinking print journalism bucket.

E-magazines were worse, paying crap. The *Huffington Post* had offered her a regular blog column, for no pay at all, which said too much about the state of that part of the industry.

Maybe she should do a piece on The Puffin Diner; there was a laugh. That was probably below even *HuffPo's* standards.

"So…" she took a deep breath and decided that since she didn't have a choice about being in town for the whole week that she'd agreed to come for anyway, she might as well put a good face on it. It wasn't like the editors of the world were in a bidding war for her next story.

She and her mother settled at a clean table beneath a watercolor painting of The Puffin Diner, one of Ma Slater's last, based on the date. "Not for Sale" was in bold type on the little card taped to the wall close beside the frame.

"So, tell me about the dress, Mom."

\# \# \#

Greg retreated. Hell, he didn't retreat, he ran away. The old Monty Python gag about "That's one nasty rabbit" came too easily to mind. Jessica Baxter was beautiful and looked all sweet and…fluffy.

Then she shoved a plate of cold food down his pants, ramming it right down inside his underwear in front of everyone. Cal Sr.'s howl of laughter had followed him right back through the service door into the side hall.

The one bathroom was occupied, so he detoured through the service door into the kitchen, his only other option.

Judge Baxter kept tending his omelets, "temperamental things omelets, can't look away from them for a second." But Greg also knew from experience that the Judge missed nothing of what happened in his restaurant.

With nowhere else to go, Greg moved over by the clean-up sink and shed the apron and his pants. At least his underwear had caught most of it. He shed those, wiped himself down with a couple of wet paper towels and pulled his pants back on commando. Greg wasn't really a commando sort of guy.

His shirt had taken the brunt of the attack. He stripped it off over his head and chucked it into the laundry bag along with his underwear and yesterday's service apron. He crossed to where he kept a spare shirt on one of the dry good storage shelves, but had never thought to keep underwear there as well. Greg yanked on the fresh shirt and buttoned it up.

"Not a word," he muttered at the Judge as he wound a fresh apron about his waist.

"The court will maintain a respectful silence at this time," the old man said with a tone as dry as week-old toast.

This and other titles are available at fine retailers everywhere.

Other works by M.L. Buchman

Angelo's Hearth
Where Dreams are Born
Where Dreams Reside
Maria's Christmas Table
Where Dreams Unfold
Where Dreams Are Written

Eagle Cove
Return to Eagle Cove
Recipe for Eagle Cove
Longing for Eagle Cove

The Night Stalkers

MAIN FLIGHT
The Night Is Mine
I Own the Dawn
Wait Until Dark
Take Over at Midnight
Light Up the Night
Bring On the Dusk
By Break of Day

WHITE HOUSE HOLIDAY
Daniel's Christmas
Frank's Independence Day
Peter's Christmas
Zachary's Christmas
Roy's Independence Day